The

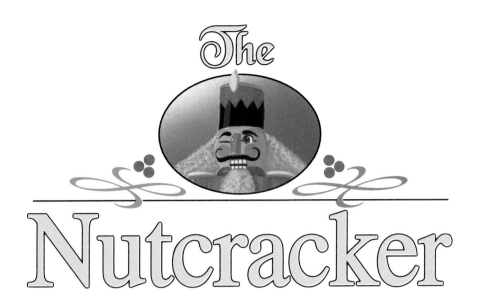

Nutcracker

retold by Mark A. Taylor
illustrated by Jim Talbot

Listen, children, and you will hear
A tale of wonder, love, and fear—
A Christmas story, filled with joy,
That started with a special toy.

It was the night Mary and her brother Fred looked forward to for months—Christmas Eve and the biggest, brightest party of the year. The aroma of freshly baked breads and puddings drifted in from the kitchen as the servants bustled about, getting ready for the evening meal.

But the children could think of only one thing.

"I wonder what Father Christmas will bring us tonight," said Mary. "Perhaps a new doll, or maybe a pretty dress."

"Oh, Mary," sighed Fred. "How boring! I want some new toy soldiers and a big wooden horse!"

Finally the waiting was over.

"Come children, come!" called their father, smiling handsomely. "Father Christmas left some gifts for you!"

Mary and Fred followed their father into the giant parlor. They couldn't help but stop in the doorway, amazed by what they saw.

A tree stood in the center of the room, twinkling with stars and covered with candy canes and popcorn and other delicious treats. But best of all—it was surrounded by presents!

The children squeezed close around their father as he handed out each bright package with a flourish.

"Aha! Look at this big one! Who could it be for? Oh, Mary, I see it has your name on it. Do you want it, Mary, or shall I give it to your brother?"

"My, oh, my, this one is heavy. I believe it weighs far too much for any child here to have. Now, let's see . . . Fred, your name is on the tag. You don't want to try to lift this awful package, do you?"

The children laughed and cheered and begged, until each gift had been opened.

And indeed, each child's wishes had been granted. Fred spent the evening breaking in his new hobby horse and preparing his troops for battle. Mary put on her new silk dress, and started to redecorate her dollhouse with the new furniture she had been given.

The children had begun to scatter from around the tree, when a heavy knocking at the door stopped all of them. The maid rushed to the entry hall and came back with a man who was at least a head shorter than the other adults in the room. His nose was long and thin, and a shiny black patch covered one eye.

"Herr Drosselmeier!" said Fred and Mary's father. "Welcome! Come in!"

"So sorry to be late," he said, breathing deeply as if he had run all the way to the party. "But I have brought something special for your Christmas. Look outside."

Now Herr Drosselmeier was the town's clockmaker, and was a very skillful craftsman. He was also the children's godfather, and every Christmas he made them a special toy with his own hands.

The children went to the front window. There before them was a beautiful castle, with moving figures and musical chimes. Miniature soldiers stood guard, and when Mary peeked through the tiny glass windows, she could see children dancing in the ballroom.

Mary and Fred watched the figures for a while, but soon found out that there was little they could do with the toy.

"Can I take the soldiers into the parlor?" Fred asked Godfather Drosselmeier. "They would make a fine addition to my regiment."

"Oh no, child. They must guard the castle," he replied.

"Do the children ever stop dancing?" asked Mary. "I should like for them to play with my doll, Miss Clara."

"Absolutely not!" said Drosselmeier, who was beginning to get cross. "I spent many days teaching these puppets to go up and down, down and up, just to amuse you."

"Oh," said Mary.

And with that, both children turned away from their godfather and went back to the Christmas tree, to play with the toys Father Christmas had given them.

"Father," called Mary, "What is this?" She pulled out a wooden statue, dressed as a soldier. It had a red jacket, purple breeches, and jet black boots.

"It's a nutcracker," he explained. He grabbed a walnut from the banquet table and inserted it in the Nutcracker's mouth. A lever behind the doll's head closed its mouth on the nut, and the shell cracked easily.

"What fun!" Mary said, clapping her hands.

"You may hold him," said Drosselmeier. But before Mary could take it, Fred grabbed the Nutcracker. He ran to a corner of the room, where he began tossing the Nutcracker into the air.

Fred's father marched to the boy and grabbed the Nutcracker in mid-air. "I'll take that!" he said with a smile. And he brought the Nutcracker to Mary who held it in her arms the rest of the evening.

Who will lose, and who will win?
Furry mice or fighting men?
Keep reading, and you'll see the way
That Mary's hero saves the day!

"Time for bed, children," said Mary's mother several hours later.

"Mother, may I stay up for a little bit longer? I still need a few minutes to put my dolls to bed. They have to have a bedtime story, you know. Please, Mother?"

"Well, alright, my dear. But don't stay up too late. We have a busy day tomorrow." And with that, Mary was left alone in the parlor.

"My poor little Nutcracker," said Mary to the little wooden creature. "Fred didn't hurt you, did he?" Mary continued to speak softly to the toy in an effort to soothe it.

And then her words stopped. The Nutcracker winked! She closed her eyes, then opened them slowly, afraid yet curious about what she would see when she looked down again. And there he was, just a wooden statue with a painted smile, looking the same as it had all evening.

"I really must go to bed," she said to herself. "Now I'm starting to see things that don't exist!"

Just as she was putting the Nutcracker on a high shelf—out of Fred's reach—she heard a strange click, click, clicking from the wooden floorboards in a far corner—and a high squeak, squeak, squeaking. It sounded to Mary just like . . . mice. Mice!

The room was crawling with mice!

"Oh!" Mary gasped. She was so afraid she couldn't move. She covered her eyes with her hands.

The room began to fill with sound. *Bong! Bong! Bong!* It was the grandfather clock, chiming midnight. *Pitter! Pitter! Patter!* It was the sound of hundreds of mice scampering across the floor! *Tinkle! Tinkle! Tinkle!* It was the sound of Mary's pull toys—the ones with bells—moving from one side of the room to the other.

Her pull toys! She peered through her fingers to look at the scene below. She couldn't believe what she saw! All of her toys had come to life—even her beloved doll, Miss Clara.

And then she heard a new sound. *Toot-to-to-toot!* It was a bugle call! She looked into the parlor and rubbed her eyes, and then she looked again.

All of Fred's soldiers—row after row of them!—now marched, with swords drawn, in a battle against the mice. And leading the army was the Nutcracker, with the longest, shiniest saber of them all!

The mice had a leader too. He looked like a king, the largest mouse in the pack, with a glistening crown on top of his head.

"Attack!" commanded the Nutcracker, and his soldiers charged forward with a mighty roar. *Clang! Clang!* With sword against sword, the battle was fierce. *Squeak! Squeak!* The Nutcracker's men fought off mouse after mouse.

"Hurrah! Hooray!" The soldiers cheered, because the Nutcracker had defeated the ugly mouse king, knocking him down and taking his crown as a symbol of triumph. He took the crown to Mary, bowed on one knee and said, "Let me make you Princess Mary, my dream come true!"

A land of magic, a land aglow,
A land where you would like to go.
A land where sweets and treats are free,
A land that Mary was able to see.

Mary had no fear of the Nutcracker. He led her through the parlor closet, and up a cedar staircase.

And there, before her eyes, was the most beautiful meadow she had ever seen. It was a glistening, glowing fairyland made of sweets.

"Where are we?" Mary asked, with wide eyes.

"We're on our way to my home!" said the Nutcracker.

They passed over Sugarcandy Meadow, went through the Almond and Raisin Gate, trampled through Christmas Tree Wood, and walked along the banks of the Orange Brook.

Soon they came to Rose Lake, so named because of the ruby red roses that grew alongside it. The scent of the flowers was overwhelming.

"We need to cross this lake to get to my home," said the Nutcracker. "Climb into this boat."

Their boat was a beautiful seashell, pulled by two dolphins. Silver fish jumped all around them, and rainbows were on the horizon.

Soon they arrived at the far shore. The Nutcracker led Mary through the city gate, into streets paved with sugar. All around them were buildings that sparkled like jewels. They even saw fountains that spouted lemonade! Mary could hardly take it all in.

Finally they reached their destination. Rock Castle. The gatekeeper let them in, and as Mary and the Nutcracker walked through the entrance, they were greeted by four beautiful women. Mary knew at once that they were princesses.

"Dear, brother—you're home!" And the ladies cried and hugged the Nutcracker all at the same time. They did not seem at all surprised that he was made of wood instead of flesh.

The Nutcracker introduced Mary to the women. "These are my sisters, Mary. And sisters, this is Mary. She helped me defeat the mouse king!"

With that announcement, a celebration broke out. The Princesses, the Nutcracker, the gatekeepers—everyone began talking at once. Mary stepped away from the confusion, just to watch the activity. She soon fell asleep, right on the castle floor.

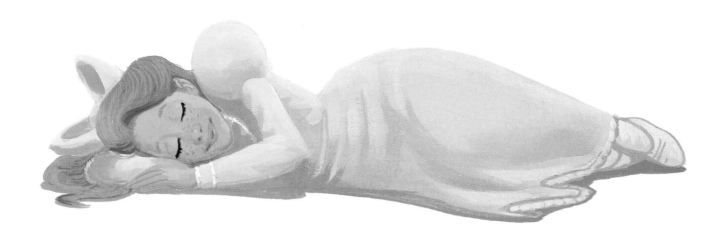

When she woke up, she was at home, on the parlor floor.

"Was I dreaming?" she said to herself.

She walked over to the toyshelf, and saw that the soldiers and dolls were in their proper places, even the Nutcracker. She picked up the little soldier.

"Ah, Nutcracker. Where did you take me? If only you were real. I would love you with all my heart!"

She put the Nutcracker back on the shelf and walked out of the room. She did not see that the words she spoke put a twinkle in his eyes and a smile on his face.

"I *am* real, Mary. I'm real in your heart."